Sekiya Miyoshi

The Promised Land

THE
PILGRIM
PRESS

Cleveland

What would it be like to move to a new home if you had to carry your own boxes for as many days as you can imagine?

A long time ago, the people of Israel were forced to work in Egypt. They had a hard, difficult life. For over 300 years, they had made mud bricks. And then they were ordered to get out of the country. Where were they going? No one could say. Suddenly their work did not seem so hard. They were afraid to go. The journey might take forever. They could only pack a few things. They had no cars or even wagons. "We are going to the land that God has promised," they were told. But they wondered.

Little Samuel certainly did not want to go. He shrieked because the green bird perched in the tree was staying. Then a man with a big beard asked Samuel, "Is the green bird your friend?" When Samuel shook his head yes, the man said, "He will come with you." Samuel's mother was relieved.

Samuel was happy. The green bird was now perched on his head as he walked through the desert.
Miriam spotted the green bird on Samuel's head. "I want that bird. I want a friend," she fussed. Her mother didn't know what to do. Then the man with the big beard came again. "Samuel and Miriam can share the walk," he said. "They can share the green bird."

Samuel and Miriam were happy together. They walked hand in hand. The green bird flew above them—or perched on their hands—while they walked in the desert.

But the way through the desert seemed endless. People got tired on the first day.

Then, look! Soldiers from Egypt were coming after them. The children cried, "Run, run. We don't want them to find us."

The people ran ahead of the soldiers—
until they came to the sea. It was wide
and seemed endless. The people of
Israel came to a stop. "What are we to
do?" they asked one another. The man
with the big beard came out. He
smacked the sea with his stick.

Were they dreaming?
The sea split itself into two parts and made a
desert road. As the people walked, the two walls
of water also moved ahead—and the desert road
seemed to stretch to the horizon. The people of
Israel walked on this marvelous road.

But the soldiers from Egypt also used the road.

Walls of water stood on both sides of this road. Many fish swam near the wall, and sometimes fish would stick their heads through the wall. "Hello, friendly fish," the children said. "Please be our friends." These children were playing on the road to the Promised Land.

The walls sometimes made pleasant waterfalls where Samuel and Miriam could play in the puddles. They had fun splashing. Then their mothers told them to hurry up. "It's so beautiful here. We don't want to keep walking." Well, the grown-ups didn't want to keep walking, either, because they were tired and gloomy.

Were they dreaming?
When their journey through the sea was completed,
the walls of water came together. Their road through
the sea to the Promised Land disappeared. And so
did the soldiers from Egypt. Ahead was a rugged
land with high mountains. All the grown ups
groaned, "Egypt was an easier place for us."

Only Samuel and Miriam were happy. They were
excited because this was their first time to climb
mountains. These were higher than the Pyramids
they built in Egypt. They began to run, but the man
with the big beard called out, "Don't go ahead so
fast!" "But, we want to run," they called back.

Samuel and Miriam stood on top of the mountain. How high they were! They stood on their tiptoes and stretched out their hands. The bearded man cried out from below, "Be careful! Or you might fall!" "But we want to touch the sky!" they called back.

They ran down the mountain and jumped into an oasis. It was so cool and refreshing that they splashed water on each other.

They played in the oasis so much that the clear water was disturbed. The bearded man scolded them again. "You shouldn't make the waters so muddy." "But, we wanted to play here. Please forgive us," the children pleaded.

A large lion approached them as they wandered through the desert. He greeted them in his own language, but it was such a loud roar that the green bird flew away. Samuel and Miriam were also frightened and ran after the bird.

This surprised the lion. He only meant to say hello. He didn't mean to scare the green bird—or the children. So he also chased after the bird. But the green bird was nowhere to be found.

Not behind the big rock. Not in the deep hole. Not among the bushes. Not even above the palm tree. Nowhere was the green bird to be seen.

Evening came. It was dark now, and stars shone in the sky. Samuel and Miriam walked slowly, sadly underneath the stars.

Suddenly, they noticed a bird-shaped star. "Has the bird become a star?" they wondered.

They walked with their eyes fixed on the bird star,
until they bumped into something big. Amazed,
they looked ahead to see the green bird perching
on a head. And the head belonged to the bearded
man.

"Sit here and let's talk," they heard a gentle voice say. They had heard this voice before, but it sounded quite different.

For a long time, they talked under the glittering stars. The bearded man's name was Moses. "Where are we going, and why?" the children asked. "To the Promised Land," said Moses, the leader of the Israelite people.

And they talked and thought about that wonderful, green Promised Land. Samuel and Miriam were eager to keep walking. They wanted to reach that Promised Land immediately. "You must help others along the way," Moses said, "because we can only reach the Promised Land together."